Amelia Bedelia

Ties the Knot

#10

Amelia Bedelia
Ties the Knot

○ + 🪢 =

by Herman Parish

pictures by Lynne Avril

← me ♥

Greenwillow Books
An Imprint of HarperCollins Publishers

Library of Congress Cataloging-in-Publication Data is available.

ISBN 978-0-06-233417-6 (hardback)—ISBN 978-0-06-233416-9 (pbk. ed.)
"Greenwillow Books."

16 17 18 19 20 CG/RRDH 10 9 8 7 6 5 4 3 2 1 First Edition

Greenwillow Books

For Julia & Chad,
expert knot-tiers—H. P.

For Chloe and Scott, who Tied the Knot . . .
15 years ago! With love—L. A.

Contents

A ~~Spring~~ sparkle in Her ~~Step~~ Eye

When Amelia Bedelia got home from school, there was a surprise waiting for her. Recognizing the car in the driveway, she jumped off her bike and ran inside. "Aunt Mary? Jason?" she hollered. "Where are you?"

"In the kitchen, sweetie!" called her mother.

1

Amelia Bedelia threw her backpack onto a chair and skipped through the living room to the kitchen. She could hear her mother and aunt talking in low voices. The only word she caught was "notices."

Amelia Bedelia ran to her aunt and gave her a giant hug.

"Hi, pussycat," said Aunt Mary. "It's wonderful to see you again."

"Pour yourself some lemonade," said Amelia Bedelia's mother. "And I'll make you a snack."

Amelia Bedelia looked around. She peeked under the breakfast table and stuck her head into the dining room. "Where's Jason?" she asked.

Amelia Bedelia hated it when her cousin jumped out from a hiding spot and surprised her. (She kind of liked the thrill too, but she would never tell anyone that.)

"Jason couldn't come," said Aunt Mary. "He just joined the track team. What's new for you in school?"

Amelia Bedelia was disappointed that her cousin wasn't there. "We just started studying flight and airplanes," she said.

3

Amelia
Earhart

"Fun! You'll hear all about Amelia Earhart," said Aunt Mary. "She was a famous aviator. She flew all over the world!"

...her plane

"Airheart is a great name for a flier," said Amelia Bedelia, "since they love to be in the air." She turned to her mother and asked, "Mom, was I named after Amelia Airheart?"

"No," said her mother, shaking her head. "It's spelled E-a-r-h-a-r-t but pronounced as Air-heart. And it would have sounded terrible to be called Earhart Bedelia."

Amelia Bedelia's mother chuckled to herself as she sliced an apple for a snack.

"Mom, just because Dad isn't here," said Amelia Bedelia, " it doesn't mean you have

4

to take his place making dumb jokes." She grabbed an apple slice and asked, "What's new with you, Aunt Mary?"

"Oh, nothing . . . ," said Aunt Mary, placing her hands palms down on the breakfast table and wiggling her fingers. Amelia Bedelia tried not to look at the huge diamond on the ring finger of Mary's left hand. Jason had told her that it was enormous, and now it was flashing and sparkling so much she practically needed sunglasses.

"Have you been back to your beach house yet?" asked Amelia Bedelia.

"Oh, yes, many times," said Mary.

"I love the beach. We had so much fun there," said Amelia Bedelia. "Do you

ever see Bob . . . Bob . . . you know, that Metal Man guy who finds stuff in the sand with his metal detector?"

"Bob Jackson," said Mary. "Actually, we see a lot of each other. We've been dating." She raised her left hand up to her face and smiled. The huge, glittery diamond ring was staring straight at Amelia Bedelia.

"Aunt Mary, you've been keeping a secret from us!" Amelia Bedelia reached across the table, grabbed Mary's left hand, and pointed at her thumbnail. "When did you get your nails painted? This red is my favorite color!"

Aunt Mary looked up at her sister, then back at Amelia Bedelia.

 "You know," said Aunt Mary. "It's gotten awfully hot in here. I may have to take off my *engagement ring*."

"You don't have to do that," said Amelia Bedelia, bounding out of her seat. "I'll open a window."

A cool breeze blew across the sunny kitchen as Amelia Bedelia sat back down.

Aunt Mary smiled. "You little stinker!" she said, laughing.

"Excuse me?" said Amelia Bedelia, but it was too late. Aunt Mary sprang out of her seat and started tickling Amelia Bedelia under her chin.

"*Ha-ha-ha*, stop it," pleaded Amelia Bedelia between gasps for air. "It was

Ha-ha-ha! Ha Ha Ha!

Jason's idea. *Hah-ha-hah-heh*—he said it would drive you bonkers!"

"Jason is an expert at that," said Aunt Mary.

"Mom, help!" yelled Amelia Bedelia.

"She is really, really ticklish under her arms," said Amelia Bedelia's mother.

Aunt Mary tickled Amelia Bedelia under the arms.

"*Ha-ha-ha-ha-ah-ha-hoo-ho!* Don't Ha Ha Ha! help Aunt Mary, Mom," gasped

Ha-ha-ha-ha-ah-ha-hoo-ho!

Ha-ha-ha! Ha-ha-ha!! *Ha-ha-ha!!*

Amelia Bedelia. "Help me!"

Amelia Bedelia was now on the floor, with Aunt Mary kneeling next to her and tickling her stomach. Amelia Bedelia rolled over, lunged up, and began tickling her mother behind her knees, her mother's most ticklish spot.

"Ohhh-nooo-ho-ho-ho!" said Amelia Bedelia's mother.

"That's exactly where I used to tickle her when we were kids!" said Aunt Mary.

"Oh, yeah?" said Amelia Bedelia's mother. She bent down and started tickling her sister's ankles. "Here's Aunt Mary's weak spot!"

"Hah-hah-hah-hah!" said Aunt Mary. *"Hah-hah-hah-hah!"*

Ha-ha-ha-ha-ah-ha

By now, all three of them were
rolling around on the floor, trying to out-
tickle and outsmart one another. Just then,
Amelia Bedelia's dog, Finally, raced into the

room, barking and spinning around. Amelia
Bedelia looked up. Her father was
standing in the doorway, slowly
shaking his head with a look of
total disbelief on his face.

Chapter 2

Massage in a Bottle

"Finally and I didn't mean to crash your teatime tickle party," said Amelia Bedelia's father.

"Oh, we were having some fun and got carried away," said Amelia Bedelia's mother, getting up off the floor. "Mary's here with some exciting news, honey. There's

going to be a wedding in the family!"

"No kidding!" said Amelia Bedelia's father as he helped Aunt Mary to her feet. "Congratulations! Have you met Jason's fiancée yet?"

Aunt Mary looked up at the ceiling and huffed. "Honestly, I feel like I have stepped into a comedy club!"

Amelia Bedelia's mother began moving in slow motion toward Amelia Bedelia's father. "His tickle spot is right under his chin," she said. "Just like Amelia Bedelia's."

Aunt Mary and Amelia Bedelia started walking toward him like zombies.

"No, no!" said Amelia Bedelia's father, backing into the family room. "I declare a tickle truce! I want to hear all about this wedding."

"I'll make us some popcorn," said Amelia Bedelia's mother. "Mary, tell him how Bob proposed to you. Honey, I'm telling you . . . you could take romance lessons from Bob."

"I'll add that to my Christmas list,"

Christmas List

said Amelia Bedelia's father, sitting back in his recliner and settling in to hear the story of Aunt Mary's engagement.

Amelia Bedelia sat on the rug, rubbing Finally's belly and listening too.

"So yesterday, right at sunset," Mary 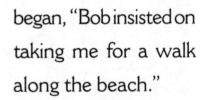 began, "Bob insisted on taking me for a walk along the beach."

"That's romantic!" called Amelia Bedelia's mother from the kitchen, over the sound of popping corn.

"Got it!" replied Amelia Bedelia's father.

"I had a feeling that Bob wanted to tell me something important,"

Aunt Mary continued. "He's so at home on the beach."

"He should move into a shell  like a hermit crab," said Amelia Bedelia.

Amelia Bedelia's father laughed. "Did Bob bring along his metal detector?" he asked.

"How did you know?" said Aunt Mary, smiling.

"Honey, that is *not* romantic," called Amelia Bedelia's father into the kitchen.

The only reply was the *pop-pop-pop* of corn.

"Anyway," said Aunt Mary, "all of a sudden Bob's headphones start buzzing, so he starts digging. He uncovers an ancient bottle with a wax seal on it. He

POP-pop-POPPity-POP!!!

15

rinses it off in the ocean, then holds it up to my ear and shakes it. Something is clinking around. Then Bob breaks the seal, turns it on its side, and out falls *this* into the palm of my hand." Aunt Mary held up her ring for Amelia Bedelia's father to see.

"Wow!" said Amelia Bedelia's father. "That is some rock!"

"That's no rock," said Amelia Bedelia. "That's a diamond."

"Diamonds are a type of rock," said her father. "In fact, the diamond is a cousin to coal, but it's put

under more heat and pressure, then cut and polished to look sparkly."

"The next time you say I'm getting coal in my stocking for Christmas, I hope it looks like that," said Amelia Bedelia. "Mary's rock rocks!"

"It must be at least a carat," said Amelia Bedelia's father.

"Almost two carats," said Mary.

"Two carrots?" said Amelia Bedelia. "That's all? Mom's got a dozen carrots in the fridge right now. Throw in a stalk of celery, a radish, and a cucumber, and you could give her a really pretty necklace, Dad."

"A diamond's weight is measured by carats," said Amelia Bedelia's father. "Its

value depends on four words that begin with the letter C—carat, color, clarity, and cut."

Amelia Bedelia's mother interrupted, handing him a big bowl of popcorn. "You forgot the fifth C—checkbook."

Amelia Bedelia's father laughed and passed the popcorn bowl to Amelia Bedelia. "Get back to Bob on the beach with the bottle," he said to Aunt Mary.

"So then Bob gets down on one knee to propose—" said Aunt Mary.

"Really romantic . . . ," said Amelia Bedelia's mother, sighing.

"Then he popped the question?" asked Amelia Bedelia's father.

Amelia Bedelia looked at the

popcorn, then back at her dad. "How do you pop a question?" she asked.

"Bob asked me to marry him," said Aunt Mary.

"Did you pop an answer?" said Amelia Bedelia.

"Yes," said Aunt Mary. "I said yes."

"Honey, here's another lesson for you," said Amelia Bedelia's mother. "Inside the bottle, Bob also put a certificate good for a day at a spa, with massage and beauty treatments included."

"Beauty treatments would be wasted on you, honey," said Amelia Bedelia's father. "You're already beautiful."

"Well, at least we agree on one thing," said Amelia Bedelia's mother, kissing him on the cheek. "You can add the money you would have spent on a spa to my diamond necklace fund."

Amelia Bedelia's father quickly changed the subject. "What does Jason think about all this?" he asked.

"Jason's very happy," said Mary. "He and Bob hang out together when we visit the shore. Bob has never forgotten how Jason and his friends saved the Beach Ball."

"You know what?" said Amelia Bedelia's mother. "We're throwing you an engagement party."

"How can you throw an entire party?" said Amelia Bedelia.

"We are?" said Amelia Bedelia's father.

"Absolutely," said Amelia Bedelia's

20

mother. "It will give the two families a chance to meet over a nice meal well before the wedding."

"How romantic," said Amelia Bedelia's father, taking her hand in his. "That reminds me of three little words I want to say to you."

Amelia Bedelia blushed. For some reason she got embarrassed when her parents said "I love you" to each other.

"What's for dinner?" Amelia Bedelia's father whispered, leaning in and looking deeply into her mother's eyes.

"Carats," said her mother, laughing and smacking him on the head. "Bunches of carats."

Chapter 3

Pop the Question

Amelia Bedelia's parents were famous for hosting fun dinner parties. Usually they didn't have a specific event to celebrate—they just got good friends together to enjoy delicious meals. Amelia Bedelia was really looking forward to this party though, because Aunt Mary's engagement was super exciting!

On the day of the party, Amelia Bedelia was in the kitchen for hours helping her mother.

"Let's take a popcorn break," suggested Amelia Bedelia's mother late in the afternoon. "I'm pooped." She poured the kernels into the popper. "You know what, sweetie?" she said. "We need something to break the ice."

"Did our fridge stop making those little cubes?" asked Amelia Bedelia.

"Gosh, I hope not," said her mother. "But when people get together for the first time, it's nice to do a fun activity. It helps everyone relax and feel comfortable."

"I can take everyone outside to play hopscotch," said Amelia Bedelia.

POP! went the first kernel. *Pop-POP!* went a couple more.

"Your grandparents probably wouldn't go for that," said Amelia Bedelia's mother, shaking her head. "My idea is a fun interview! I made a list of questions for Mary and Bob to answer. That way, they can tell us everything at the same time, without having to repeat themselves all night."

"Sounds like you're giving them a test," said Amelia Bedelia.

POP-pop-POPPITY-POP! went the popcorn.

"There's got to be a fun way to ask questions," said Amelia Bedelia's mother. "Like when Bob—"

Popped the question!

"Popped the question!" said Amelia Bedelia and her mother at the same time. They hugged, congratulating themselves for being geniuses.

The popcorn agreed. *POP! POP! POP! POP! POP! POP!!!*

"I have an idea," said Amelia Bedelia's mother. "We can write questions on little strips of paper, like the fortunes in fortune cookies, and stick them in popcorn."

"Neat! Oh, but the corn has already popped," said Amelia Bedelia. "What else pops?"

Her mother thought for a second, then said, "I bought balloons to decorate the house . . ."

"Perfect!" said Amelia Bedelia. "We'll

25

put a question inside each balloon, blow the balloons up, take a pin, and—*POP!* They get a question."

Amelia Bedelia adored questions. Whenever she didn't know what to do or say next, she would ask a question. Her mother's list had good questions that people would like to know the answers to. Amelia Bedelia added a few more, some mysteries she had always wondered about. Then she cut out the questions, rolled each strip of paper into a little cylinder, and inserted the cylinders into the balloons.

Does Bob always carry his metal detector with him?

What is your favorite book?

Is there a date for the wedding?

Who is the BEST MAN?

What's your favorite thing about Mary?

Where will you go on the honeymoon?

Where did you grow up?

Does Bob always wear that baseball cap?

The first to arrive was Amelia Bedelia's aunt Wanda, her father's older sister. Not bothering with the bell, she bounded through the open door, with Finally barking happily at her heels, and bellowed, "I'm here! Let the party begin!"

Aunt Wanda was delighted with the Pop the Question icebreaker idea. She convinced Amelia Bedelia's father to blow up the balloons, saying, "I hope they don't float away, with all your hot air."

Once he had finished and tied them off, Wanda used a marker to draw a huge question mark on each one. Then Amelia Bedelia put all the balloons in a big bag, ready to be popped.

Amelia Bedelia's father was out of breath when he opened the door for Grandma and Granddad, who arrived at the same time as Mary, Bob, Jason, and Bob's brother, Tom. There were hugs and kisses all around. Amelia Bedelia and Jason began jumping and dancing

together in a wild circle until
they both tripped and fell
down laughing. They'd
been greeting each other this same way
since they were little kids.

"Grandma, I'll bet you're happy that
Mary is getting married," said Amelia
Bedelia's father.

"Finally!" said Grandma.

"Mother, shush!" said Aunt Mary.

"What's wrong?" said Grandma, pointing
at Finally. "Isn't that her name? Come here,
sweet puppy! Say hello to Grandma."

Finally scampered over, wagging her tail.

"You know," said Grandma. "It took me
a while too, but I finally found Mr. Right."

"Yup," said Granddad. "And when she

29

did, she couldn't decide between Orville or Wilbur, so she married me."

Amelia Bedelia's grandfather and father started laughing.

"Wait. Grandma. You knew the Wright brothers?" said Amelia Bedelia. "You need to come talk to my class, we're studying aviation pioneers and . . ."

Now everyone was laughing, except for Amelia Bedelia.

"R-i-g-h-t," said Jason, flicking her ear. "Right, not Wright."

While Amelia Bedelia's mother served yummy little things to eat and her father took care of soft drinks, Amelia Bedelia told Aunt Mary and Bob how to play Pop the Question. She gave a pin to Bob, and he

Wright
brothers

POPPED the first balloon. He snatched the piece of paper out of midair and unrolled the question. "'Do you two have a date for the wedding?'" he read out loud.

"They don't need dates," said Amelia Bedelia. "They have each other."

"Finally!" said Grandma loudly.

Finally trotted over to Grandma and licked her fingers.

Aunt Mary smiled. "We're still deciding. Once we do, we'll send out save-the-date cards."

POP went a question. Bob read, "'Who is the best man?'"

"Bob is," said Amelia Bedelia. "If there were someone better, she'd be marrying him instead."

31

"I agree," said Aunt Mary.

"Thanks for that vote of confidence," said Bob. "My older brother, Tom here, will be my best man."

POP went a question. Mary read, "'Does Bob always wear that baseball cap?'"

Everyone laughed. Amelia Bedelia's mother arched one eyebrow at her daughter, but Amelia Bedelia didn't care. She really wanted to know.

"No," said Bob. "I have many caps, so I like to rotate them."

Amelia Bedelia was happy to have this information. She had no idea why people were laughing.

POP went a question. Aunt Mary said, "Uh-oh, I dropped the pin."

"Bob can find it with his metal detector," said Granddad.

"That's the next question," said Aunt Mary. "'Does Bob always carry his metal detector with him?'"

"Of course not," said Bob. "It's in the trunk of my car."

Another good answer, thought Amelia Bedelia, even though her mother was arching both eyebrows at her.

"Just don't bring it to the wedding," said Aunt Mary, laughing.

Chapter 4

Something Old, Something New . . .

Aunt Mary had invited Amelia Bedelia to help her pick out a wedding dress. It was a full car! Amelia Bedelia sat between her grandma and Aunt Wanda. Amelia Bedelia's mother was driving, with Aunt Mary beside her.

"Let's start in the mall, at the bridal shop," suggested

34

Amelia Bedelia's mother.

"Mom, a bridle is for a horse," said Amelia Bedelia.

"How about a harness," said Grandma with a chuckle, "so Mary and Bob can get hitched."

Aunt Mary laughed. "Maybe I won't wear a dress at all."

"You're going to get married in your pj's?" said Amelia Bedelia.

"No, silly," said Aunt Mary. "I'll wear nice pants."

Grandma made a face. "You should look like a princess," she said.

"Or a goddess," said Amelia Bedelia's mother. "I'll never forget the look on Bob's face when he

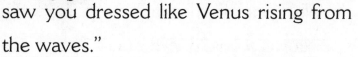

saw you dressed like Venus rising from the waves."

"Wow," said Aunt Wanda. "Venus the goddess sounds like a good plan to me. Maybe I'll come to the wedding as Venus the planet!"

The ladies were still laughing as they walked into Head Over Heels, the bridal shop in the mall. Amelia Bedelia looked around in amazement. She couldn't believe how many white dresses there were in every style, shape, length, and size imaginable. There were even gowns hanging from the ceiling!

"Welcome, ladies," said a saleswoman. "My name is Sylvie. Who is the lucky bride?"

"My aunt is," said Amelia Bedelia, pointing at Aunt Mary.

"Congratulations," said Sylvie, smiling at Aunt Mary. "What did you have in mind?"

"I'm thinking goddess, with a dash of princess," said Aunt Mary.

"Hmmm," said Sylvie. "That's a tall order."

"She's not that tall," said Amelia Bedelia, looking at the ceiling and the

gowns that floated like clouds above her.

"Would you like a dress with a train?" asked Sylvie.

"Good idea," said Amelia Bedelia. "She's marrying an engineer."

Aunt Mary tried on a dozen dresses at Head Over Heels, but none of them fit the bill. She tried on five more dresses at Made in Heaven, six at Wedding Bells Are Ringing, and another ten at Puppy Love, but those weren't right, either.

Some dresses had trains, others did not. Some came with veils, and one even featured five thousand tiny pearls sewn into the skirt.

38

"It's an emotional decision," said Aunt Wanda. "Listen to your gut."

Just then, Amelia Bedelia's stomach growled loudly. She blushed.

"Who growled?" said Grandma, looking around. "Is that sweet Finally here?"

Amelia Bedelia's stomach growled even louder.

"Amelia Bedelia," said Aunt Wanda, "don't you ever feed that thing?"

"She's just trying to help," said Amelia Bedelia's mother. "Maybe her gut will tell Mary which dress to get."

"Let's have lunch," said Aunt Wanda. "It won't be an official girls' outing unless we do."

"We're almost at the beach," said Aunt Mary. "There's a great café right over the causeway, near the harbor. They make yummy sandwiches for picnics. Bob and I love it. It's our place."

Just then, Wanda yelled, "Stop! There it is! That's the place my friend told me about!"

As her mother pulled over, Amelia

Bedelia read the sign on the weather-beaten building. "Second Helpings? Does this place serve leftovers?"

"You could say that," said Aunt Wanda. "But it's not a restaurant. It's a vintage clothing shop."

"Used clothes?" said Grandma with a frown.

"Previously worn," said Aunt Wanda. "Stylish clothes at bargain prices." She led the way inside and introduced herself to the owner.

Amelia Bedelia fell in love with the shop immediately. She saw clothes in every style and color and fabric. There were dresses from yesterday and from a hundred years ago.

"You don't have wedding dresses, do you?" asked Aunt Mary.

"Just one," said Lois, the owner. "And it's a beauty. Got it last week at an estate sale."

"Where did you put the estate?" asked

Amelia Bedelia, looking around at the jam-packed shop.

Lois smiled. "I only bought the dress. I couldn't resist it," she said.

Neither could Mary, once she saw it. She almost ran to the fitting room. She emerged a few minutes later, looking stunning.

"Move over, Venus," Amelia Bedelia's

mother said, helping Aunt Mary tie a big satin bow.

"That's handmade lace over silk," said Lois. "It's from the 1930s."

"It's perfect," said Aunt Mary.

Amelia Bedelia's stomach growled like a bear.

"Hear that?" said Aunt Wanda. "A genuine gut reaction."

"Everyone in the county could hear it!" said Grandma.

Amelia Bedelia blushed bright red as her mother said, "We've got to get some lunch into you, sweetie."

Chapter 5

Bride-to-Be, or Not to Be

"Well," said Aunt Mary as everyone piled back into the car. "I'm halfway there. My dress is old, and I'll get new shoes to match it."

"Now you need something borrowed and something blue," said Aunt Wanda.

Amelia Bedelia's mother glanced at Amelia Bedelia in the rearview mirror.

"It's an old saying, sweetie," she said. "If a bride wears something old, something new, something borrowed, and something blue, then she'll have good luck."

"That didn't work the first time I got married," said Aunt Mary.

"You didn't have a wedding the first time," said Grandma.

"Your aunt eloped, honey," said Amelia Bedelia's mother.

"What antelope?" said Amelia Bedelia. Her mother wasn't making any sense at all. "I've got a teddy bear, a monkey, and a bunny."

Aunt Mary laughed and said, "I'm your aunt, and I eloped. I married my

46

first husband, Jason's father, down at city hall with just a judge and a witness."

"You don't need a big ceremony with food and music and dancing or even a white dress to get married," said Aunt Wanda.

"Humpf," said Grandma.

"You just need an official and a license," said Amelia Bedelia's mother.

"You need a license to get married?" said Amelia Bedelia. "Like for driving?"

"It's the law," said Grandma.

At last they drove onto the causeway to the beach. As Amelia Bedelia was getting hungrier and hungrier, the traffic was getting slower and slower. Finally their car came to a complete stop. She looked out the window. She could see all kinds of boats on the water, from sailboats to a huge freighter.

"Bad timing," said Amelia Bedelia's mother.

"Uh-oh," said Aunt Mary. "Drawbridge."

"No paper," said Amelia Bedelia.

"Amelia Bedelia," said Aunt Mary, "see how that section of the causeway bridge is raised?"

"Yup," said Amelia Bedelia.

"We've never seen the bridge up, in all the times we've been on the island.

It's letting ships that are taller than the bridge pass through," said her mother.

Up ahead, Amelia Bedelia saw the top of the freighter pass by. Minutes later, the drawbridge lowered into place and the cars continued on.

"There's the café," said Aunt Mary, pointing ahead. "Let's eat!"

As Amelia Bedelia's mother slowed down to make the turn into the parking lot, the front door of the café swung open and a man walked out.

"Isn't that Bob?" she asked.

It was Bob. He was wearing a baseball cap like always. And he was carrying a picnic basket and holding the door for the woman who walked out after him. She had dark, curly hair and dangly earrings that flashed in the sun. The two of them were laughing.

"Who's that with him?" asked Aunt Mary.

Amelia Bedelia's mother parked the car, and they all watched as Bob and the woman walked onto the pier. Bob helped

the woman step down into a speedboat. She started the engine. Bob cast off the lines, and they went racing across the bay.

No one said a word. It was like they had all been watching a movie together. Amelia Bedelia's mother faced Mary, and Mary turned to face her sister. Then they both turned to look back at Amelia Bedelia. Their eyes were glistening. Amelia Bedelia decided that asking a question would not be a good idea. She wished for someone, anyone, to break this silence.

Amelia Bedelia looked out the car window. A girl was walking up the pier. *Wait a minute.* Amelia Bedelia knew her!

"Pearl!" Amelia Bedelia yelled.

Pearl had taught Amelia Bedelia how to sail. Pearl was the best!

"Mom, can I get out, please?" she said. "It's Pearl!"

"What about lunch?" said Amelia Bedelia's mother. "Let's eat!"

"I'm not hungry anymore," said Amelia Bedelia. "I'm just going to go say hi to Pearl, okay? Please?"

Her mother said something to Aunt Mary, but Amelia Bedelia couldn't make it out. "Okay, sweetie," said Amelia Bedelia's mother. "Come right back.

We'll be in the café waiting for you."

"Pearl!" Amelia Bedelia yelled as she hopped out of the car.

Pearl looked up and dropped her duffel bag. "Amelia Bedelia!" she hollered, and began running to greet her. They hugged so hard that they nearly knocked each other over. "What are you doing here?"

"I was having a great day, until I wasn't," said Amelia Bedelia. "Please, please, can we take a sail?"

"Sure!" said Pearl.

Amelia Bedelia's stomach growled. "Got anything to eat? I'm starving."

Pearl searched her pockets and pulled out a broken granola bar. Amelia Bedelia devoured it as they climbed aboard Pearl's sailboat, the *Mother-and-Father-of-Pearl*.

"Okay," said Pearl. "Remember how to cast off?"

"Aye, aye," said Amelia Bedelia. "Let's get out of here!"

Pearl cupped her hand around her mouth to imitate a train conductor. "Next stop, Blackberry Island!" she called.

Chapter 6

A Knotty Lesson

Amelia Bedelia hoisted the sail. Instantly, a gust of wind filled it with a reassuring *pop*. The sound reminded her of all the fun they'd had playing Pop the Question at the engagement party. That seemed like a million years ago. Amelia Bedelia felt as if she'd learned more today than she ever had in school. Way more than she even wanted to know, really. Being a grown-up sure didn't seem like much fun to her.

Amelia Bedelia sat down beside Pearl, who was steering a course for Blackberry Island, the small island in the middle of the bay. Pearl, Jason, and Amelia Bedelia had named it after they'd discovered gobs of juicy blackberries growing there. That seemed like a billion years ago.

She told Pearl about shopping for a wedding dress, and how upset her aunt Mary had been when she'd seen Bob with a picnic basket and the other woman. Why was he going on a picnic with someone else when he was about to marry Aunt Mary?

"Yipes," said Pearl. "Sounds stressful."
She handed a piece of rope to Amelia
Bedelia. It was the same thickness as the
line used for hoisting the sail, but only
about six feet long.

"What's this for?" asked Amelia
Bedelia, holding it up.

"Well," said Pearl, "if you're going to
get tied up in knots, you ought to know
what you're doing, right? Here's a basic
knot to tie a boat to a pier. A round turn
with two half hitches." She looped the
line around a block of wood twice and
made one half hitch, then another. Then
it was Amelia Bedelia's turn.

"Perfect," said Pearl. "Now try it with one hand."

"One-handed?" said Amelia Bedelia.

Pearl nodded. "In rough weather, one hand will be busy holding the boat steady while the other hand ties the two half hitches, securing the boat to the pier."

Amelia Bedelia tied the knot using only her right hand. She did it again. And again. And again.

"Yippee!" yelled Amelia Bedelia on her fourth try.

"Great job," said Pearl. "Once more, with your eyes shut."

"What? Why?"

"At night, you might need

58

one hand for steering and one hand for tying. You can't grow a third hand to hold a flashlight. You've got to have a feel for it."

Amelia Bedelia closed her eyes and got to work. Although she had her eyes shut, a movie was playing in her head. She imagined how the line should feel, twisting and turning, making first one, then two half hitches.

"Bravo," said Pearl. "And that is just one knot. There are hundreds of different knots."

"I thought there were just ten," said Amelia Bedelia.

"Ten!" said Pearl. "What gave you that idea?"

"The signs all over the marina," said Amelia Bedelia. "The ones that say

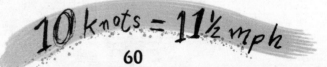
10 knots = 11½ mph

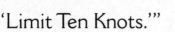

'Limit Ten Knots.'"

Pearl laughed. "That type of knot measures speed. It means *nautical* miles per hour. A nautical mile on the water is a little longer than a mile on land."

"So those signs saying 'Limit Ten Knots' . . ." Amelia Bedelia was still confused.

"That's actually about eleven and a half miles per hour on land. Going faster makes a wave; we call it the *wake*. That causes tied-up boats to knock against the pier and get damaged."

Pearl sailed closer to Blackberry Island. Amelia Bedelia could just see the roof of the deserted cottage in the middle of the island. But what got her attention was a brand-new dock extending into the water. A speedboat was tied to it.

"Perfect!" said Amelia Bedelia. "I'll try a round turn with two half hitches."

"Let's anchor around the other side instead, and wade ashore," said Pearl. "Those people in the boat could be pirates." She laughed. "That's the beauty of sailing—the boat is silent and you can be sneaky."

They dropped the anchor, waded ashore, and began walking toward the cottage. When they got close, Amelia Bedelia and Pearl began crawling on their hands and knees, slinking silently through the bushes like a pair of stalking tigers. They considered themselves experts at sneaking up on people. Together they had snuck up on Jason and his pirate buddies, overhearing their plans to disrupt the annual Beach Ball.

"See?" said Amelia Bedelia. "The cottage looks just like it did when we left it, except the blackberries aren't ripe yet this year. There's no one here."

Then a voice boomed behind them. "Hey, you kids! What are you doing on my island?"

Chapter 7

"Hey, You Kids!"

Amelia Bedelia had often wondered how she would react in a scary situation. She was sure she would stay calm. Keep cool. Be courageous.

But at the sound of that man's voice, Amelia Bedelia screamed "YEE-AHHH!" and leaped into Pearl's arms like a baby. Her dog, Finally, had done the

Yee-ahhhh!!!

Yee-ahhhh!!

same thing the first time she'd heard thunder. Amelia Bedelia buried her face in Pearl's shoulder. When she heard loud laughter, she looked up.

A man wearing a baseball cap was bent over double, trying to catch his breath. He was laughing so hard the leaves on the trees were practically shaking. Amelia Bedelia could not see his face, just the top of his cap. Standing next to him was a lady who was clearly amused by the man's reaction. Her dangly earrings flashed in the sun.

It suddenly dawned on Amelia Bedelia that this was the same woman she'd seen with Bob Jackson outside the café.

That's when the man finally straightened up and said, "I'm sorry I scared you, Amelia Bedelia! But you should have seen the look on your face!" Bob took off his glasses and wiped tears of laughter out of his eyes.

"I'm putting you down, Amelia Bedelia," said Pearl. She was laughing too.

Amelia Bedelia began laughing at herself and how ridiculous she must have looked in Pearl's arms.

"What are you doing here?" asked

Bob. "How did you get here?"

"A boat," said Amelia Bedelia.

"I mean," said Bob, "what brought you back down to the shore?"

"A car," said Amelia Bedelia.

Bob smiled and shook his head. Amelia Bedelia smiled back. She was relieved, because so far, she hadn't told any fibs. She looked at Pearl and opened her eyes really wide. Pearl nodded as if to say, Good job, and yes, this is so weird!

"Well," said Bob, "I'm glad you're here, whatever the reason."

"We were afraid we were trespassing," said Pearl.

"You are trespassers!" said Bob in his loud mean-man voice.

"It's too late to scare us now," said Amelia Bedelia.

Bob smiled. "Actually, this island does belong to me. It's been in our family for generations. See that crumbling cottage? My great-grandfather built it by hand."

"Wow," said Pearl. "I've been sailing around here for years. It's always deserted. I've never thought about someone owning it."

"Well, you two stumbled across our little secret," said Bob. He winked at the

lady with the flashing earrings, and she smiled. "You've got to promise not to say a word to Mary about this."

There was an awkward silence as Amelia Bedelia looked at Pearl and Pearl looked back at Amelia Bedelia. Then Bob hit his forehead with the heel of his hand, as though he had just remembered something important.

"I'm so sorry," he said. "Where are my manners? I'd like you to meet Anita

Jackson. She's my niece, the daughter of my older brother, Tom."

Amelia Bedelia felt like a ten-ton weight had been lifted from her shoulders.

"It's so so so so great to meet you," she said to Anita. "I'm Amelia Bedelia, and this is my friend Pearl."

"Come on into the cottage," said Bob, holding back the thorny blackberry canes so they could pass. "I want to show you something."

"This is where we got the blackberries for the cobbler," said Amelia Bedelia. "The one Aunt Mary accidentally baked her ring in."

"I found the ring with my metal detector," said Bob to Anita.

"Metal Man to the rescue!" Anita laughed. "That's our nickname for Uncle Bob," she explained.

"Hey! That's what we call him too!" said Amelia Bedelia.

"When I placed that ring back on Mary's finger," said Bob, "I realized that what I'd actually found was the one for me."

Amelia Bedelia opened her eyes wide again and looked at Pearl. She wished Aunt Mary could hear this.

They gathered around an old table in the messy dining room. The table was covered with plans and drawings. "Anita's an architect," said Bob. "She's drawn up the plans for

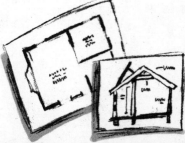

a major renovation of the cottage. This is going to be my wedding present for Mary and Jason!"

Wow! Amelia Bedelia knew that her aunt and cousin would love that. Her stomach growled loudly.

"We've got some sandwiches," said Bob, opening the picnic basket. "Let's have lunch while Anita shows you the plans. We're going to have solar power and . . ."

Lunch! Oh, no! Amelia Bedelia had told her mother that she'd be right back!

"My mom's waiting for me," said Amelia Bedelia. "But the cottage is great! Could we take two sandwiches with us instead?" She grabbed Pearl's hand. "Bye and thank you! Nice meeting you, Anita!"

"Remember," Bob called out. "Don't breathe a word to Mary or Jason!"

"We promise!" yelled Pearl.

"Cross our hearts!" hollered Amelia Bedelia as she and Pearl raced back to the sailboat, sandwiches in hand.

Chapter 8

Stormy Weather

Pearl and Amelia Bedelia sailed back to the marina in record time. It was not soon enough for Amelia Bedelia's mother. She was standing on the pier with her hands on her hips. She did not look happy.

"I know, I know," said Amelia Bedelia, tying up the sailboat with her first official knot, a round turn and two half hitches. She was thinking that if she owned up to making a mistake, her mother would be more understanding.

"Young lady . . . ," said Amelia Bedelia's mother.

Amelia Bedelia knew that this was not a good sign. Whenever a grown-up called her a young lady, it was the tip of an iceberg threatening to sink the good ship *Amelia Bedelia*. She and Pearl hopped out of the boat and onto the pier.

"Young lady," said her mother once again. "Welcome back."

"Thanks, Mom," said Amelia Bedelia. She gave her mom a hug. Maybe she was going to get off easy after all.

"I hope you enjoy dry land," said Amelia Bedelia's mother. "Because you are grounded!"

"Mom!" wailed Amelia Bedelia.

"It was my fault," said Pearl. "We were having fun, and I lost track of time."

"You are a good friend, Pearl, and you're a good sailor," said Amelia Bedelia's mother. "But my daughter needs to learn a lesson. She can't just take off and not tell anyone where she is going or when she is coming back."

Amelia Bedelia hung her head. She felt really bad that she had worried her mother.

"Sweetie, I was about to call the coast guard to search for you two!"

Now Amelia Bedelia felt like crying.

"We'd better head back," called Aunt Wanda, jogging down the pier toward them. "Mary wants to stop by Second Helpings on our way to see if she can return the dress."

Amelia Bedelia looked up. "Did Aunt Mary find a dress she liked better?"

Amelia Bedelia's mother and Aunt

Wanda glanced at each other, then back at Amelia Bedelia. "Sweetie—" said her mother.

"Mary changed her mind," said Aunt Wanda. "There isn't going to be a wedding."

"No wedding!" said Amelia Bedelia. "But Bob has worked so hard!" She clapped her hands over her mouth.

"What about Bob?" said Amelia Bedelia's mother.

"Did you see Bob?" asked Aunt Wanda. "Come on, you let the cat out of the bag. Spill the beans, already."

Amelia Bedelia and Pearl looked at each other. "I didn't spill any beans out of a bag with a cat," said Amelia Bedelia.

"Would you excuse us for a second?" Pearl said. She grabbed Amelia Bedelia and pulled her down the pier. "We promised Bob not to tell your aunt Mary," she said. "Can't we tell your mom as long as she doesn't give away the surprise? It's our only chance to save the wedding."

Amelia Bedelia agreed. The first thing she did was swear her mother and Aunt Wanda to secrecy. Then she and Pearl told them the whole story. By the time they got back to the parking lot to meet Grandma and Aunt Mary, they had a plan.

"I'm so sorry, Amelia Bedelia," said Aunt Mary. "It's such a beautiful dress and I know you were excited. But it's easier to call off a wedding than a marriage. Believe me, I know."

"You can't do that, Aunt Mary," said Amelia Bedelia.

"I'm so sorry, sweetie," said Aunt Mary.

"You really can't call off the wedding," said Amelia Bedelia.

"Why not?" asked Aunt Mary.

"I can't tell you," said Amelia Bedelia. She glanced at her mother and Aunt Wanda. They both nodded.

Aunt Mary looked at them. She was frowning.

"This should be an interesting ride home," said Grandma.

When Pearl hugged Amelia Bedelia good-bye, she whispered, "We survived the hurricane!"

Luckily for Amelia Bedelia, her mom, grandma, and aunts had barely touched their lunches. Everyone had a box of

 leftovers in the car.

Amelia Bedelia's stomach was still growling a little.

"Want to dig in to my doggie bag?" asked Grandma.

Amelia Bedelia opened Grandma's box. "I don't eat dogs, Grandma, but I'll eat this grilled cheese," she said. "And the pickle!"

After Amelia Bedelia had devoured most of the four lunches, she dozed off. Leaning her head against Grandma for a pillow, she dreamed of tying knots at ten knots per hour.

Chapter 9

Go with the Flo

By the time they returned to Amelia Bedelia's house, the wedding was back on. Amelia Bedelia, who had slept the entire way home, hoped that her mother and Aunt Wanda had kept the promise that Amelia Bedelia had made to Bob. Whatever they'd said had certainly worked.

"One last thing," said Aunt Wanda.

Everyone was still sitting in the car. "You'll have less stress if you hire someone who does weddings for a living."

"That's a job?" said Amelia Bedelia. "Getting married?"

"You can't make a career of being a bride," said Aunt Wanda, laughing. "But planning a wedding is a big job."

"Can you recall the name of that planner you were raving about?" said Aunt Mary.

Aunt Wanda shook her head and said, "Not at the moment, but she's perfect."

"Maybe I'll have a destination wedding," said Aunt Mary.

Amelia Bedelia's mother sighed dreamily. "Yes! And go somewhere romantic!"

"Like Italy," said Aunt Mary. "Maybe Venice. Or Florence."

"That's it!" said Aunt Wanda.

Aunt Mary laughed. "Is Florence your pick?"

"No, that's the wedding planner's name! Florence," said Wanda. "She goes by Flo."

"Flo?" said Grandma.

"Flo does everything," said Wanda. "Her slogan is 'Go with the Flo.'"

"Sounds like you can relax, Mary," said Amelia Bedelia's mother, "and enjoy being the bride."

Aunt Wanda was not kidding. The very next day, Amelia Bedelia was playing catch

Go with the flow

with Jason in her front yard when a sports car skidded to a stop at the curb. The door swung open, and out sprang Florence, the wedding planner. She bounded up to

the front door, her jewelry jangling. She looked and sounded like she was moving even when she was standing still.

By the time Amelia Bedelia and Jason got to the living room, Flo was pacing to and fro, lecturing Aunt Wanda, Aunt

Mary, and Amelia Bedelia's mother, who were squished together on the coach.

"Leave everything to me," said Flo. "But as I warn all my brides—don't expect perfection! Things will go wrong, as they always do. I guarantee it!"

"Oh, no," whispered Jason to Amelia Bedelia. "That doesn't sound good."

"Years from now," continued Flo as she swished back and forth across the living room

rug, "you'll look back and those little catastrophes will be what makes your wedding special and unique. I guarantee that too! And at the end of the day, you'll be married."

Amelia Bedelia whispered back, "Sounds wonderful. Even the goof-ups will be great."

Flo handed out sheets of paper. There were questions to be answered and all kinds of diagrams and lists. "These are my Flo charts," she said. "Fill these in, and they will keep us on track for the big day. First off, who is the maid of honor?"

Amelia Bedelia couldn't believe it. A maid of honor?

Aunt Mary grabbed Amelia Bedelia's mother by the wrist and raised her hand. "Here's my matron of honor," she said.

Aunt Mary is the best, thought Amelia Bedelia. *Now Mom won't have to clean up after the wedding!*

"And who are your bridesmaids?" asked Flo.

Aunt Mary raised
Wanda's hand. "Here's
one," she said.

Amelia Bedelia
couldn't imagine that! Aunt
Wanda hated housework.
Amelia Bedelia raised her hand.
"I'm good with a vacuum," she
said. "I can help."

Flo looked at Amelia Bedelia.
"You'd be a fantastic flower girl."
"What kind of flower?" she asked.
"Wild," said Flo. "I'll bring you a bunch
on the big day."

Chapter 10
~~Bachelor~~ Bachelorette Slumber Party ~~Boat~~

The one thing, *two* things, that Flo the wedding planner refused to handle were the bachelor and bachelorette parties— the traditional parties for the groom and the bride, given by their friends.

Aunt Mary decided that she wanted an old-fashioned slumber party at her beach house. That was when Amelia Bedelia's

BAHHHHHNNN

father said, "The best way to escape the bridal brigade is to go to sea."

"To see what?" asked Amelia Bedelia.

"To see how many huge fish we can catch," said her father.

Amelia Bedelia's father planned a deep-sea fishing trip for the guys on the same night as the bachelorette slumber party. Captain Will was going to take them out on the *Reel Busy*.

♥♥♥

92

Amelia Bedelia and her mother were sad to see them go, but also delighted to get rid of them for a night. They got busy in the kitchen making all of Aunt Mary's favorite dishes, such

as macaroni and cheese, lasagna, and chicken pot pie. For

lasagna!

chicken pot pie!

dessert, Amelia Bedelia's mother arranged for a pastry chef to bring different wedding cakes and icings to sample. Aunt Mary wanted everyone to taste each cake and icing and vote on the most delicious combinations so that she could tell Flo what kind of cake to order.

"Eating cakes and grading them is the kind of homework

macaroni and cheese!

mini wedding cakes!

I like," said Amelia Bedelia.

Everyone sat around the living room sampling cake and telling stories. Amelia Bedelia's mother told Amelia Bedelia's favorite story about her parents. How they had rented a camper for their honeymoon and spent the entire time getting themselves out of one pickle after another, including mud puddles, a beehive, and an encounter with an angry moose.

"My brand-new husband kept his sense of humor throughout the whole ordeal," said Amelia Bedelia's mother. "He kept laughing, and he kept me laughing. That's when I knew I had married the right guy."

94

When Aunt Mary turned on her favorite romantic movie, something about couples getting mixed up on an ocean liner and the captain marrying them, Amelia Bedelia fell asleep.

Early the next morning, Amelia Bedelia, Amelia Bedelia's mother, Aunt Wanda, Aunt Mary, and Grandma were having French toast and fruit when Amelia Bedelia's father, Granddad, and Jason came home. They were tired but happy.

"How was it, guys?" asked Aunt Mary.

"We caught a whopper," said Amelia

Bedelia's father as he kissed his daughter on top of her head. "We hooked this monster fish right away."

"Yeah," said Jason. "We took turns fighting it. We had to strap ourselves into a chair, or we would've gotten pulled overboard. It took us hours to land."

"A whopper, huh?" said Amelia Bedelia's mother. "Where is it?"

"Wow!" said Amelia Bedelia. "Can I see it?"

"It's on its way to Japan," said Granddad.

"Japan!" said Amelia Bedelia.

"It was a bluefin tuna," said her father. "Once we got it aboard the *Reel Busy*, Captain Will alerted a fishing boat that buys high-quality fish for sushi."

"It was really cool," said Jason. "Bluefin tuna are so valuable that the people who buy them can afford to put them on a plane to Tokyo! They'll auction the tuna off in the morning."

Amelia Bedelia and her mother burst out laughing. Grandma, Aunt Wanda, and Aunt Mary were

sushi

97

Bluefin Tuna

laughing too.

"Dad," said Amelia Bedelia. "The only whopper is that story."

"Pretty fishy," said her mother. "You had me going for a minute."

"Next time catch a flying fish," said Amelia Bedelia. "It can fly itself to Japan." She began giggling.

"I must admit," said Amelia Bedelia's mother, "you three had your story down. Good job keeping your faces straight!"

Granddad, Jason, and Amelia Bedelia's father looked at one another, then back at the ladies. They weren't laughing. They weren't smiling either.

"Oh, I almost forgot," said Amelia Bedelia's father, pulling

a wad of money
out of his pocket. "Here's your
share, Jason."

Amelia Bedelia had never seen a
hundred-dollar bill before.

Her father began counting quietly.
"One, two, three, four, five, six, seven,
eight, nine, and . . . ten."

Amelia Bedelia and her mother were
speechless.

"Thanks!" said Jason.

"And here's your share, Granddad."
He began counting quietly again.

Grandma's mouth made a perfect O.

Amelia Bedelia's father
handed the rest of the
money to Amelia Bedelia's

mother. "Add this to your diamond necklace fund," he said. "By the way, what did you ladies accomplish while we were gone?"

"We helped Aunt Mary decide which wedding cake to get," said Amelia Bedelia.

"Don't tell me," said Amelia Bedelia's father. "That's my favorite kind of surprise."

Chapter 11

Stuck Up

The wedding was all set for a Saturday afternoon. Bob and Mary had decided to get married on the beach, in the exact same spot where they'd first met and where Bob had proposed.

Mary's beach house was close by, so it became headquarters for the event. Flo arrived early with a clipboard and

pages and

pages of checklists.

She cleared the coffee and doughnuts off the kitchen table and spread out a huge diagram. There were checklists for events, menus, numbers and clocks, circles around names, and photographs of everyone involved—family, guests, and helpers. Red arrows were shooting every which way.

"This is my master Flo chart," said Flo. "If everything goes perfectly, this is how it will unfold."

"You just unfolded it," said Amelia Bedelia.

"I mean—" Flo's phone rang. "Hold on, honey, I need to stay in

touch with about twenty people until the *I do*s are all done." Flo's smile vanished. "Hello? Yes, it's me. Yes, I'm here." Her eyes grew bigger and bigger.

Jason leaned over to Amelia Bedelia and whispered, "The last time I saw eyes like that, a car had accidentally run over a frog."

Amelia Bedelia almost spit out her juice. She shivered at the thought.

"Stuck *up*?" yelled Flo into her

phone. "What do you mean, stuck up? Are you kidding me?"

Every adult in the kitchen took a sip of coffee and pretended not to hear Flo. But everyone was listening to every word.

"I don't think she's stuck up," Amelia Bedelia whispered to Jason. "Do you?"

"Call you right back," said Flo. Turning to Mary, she said. "What's the story with this drawbridge of yours? They raised it, but now it won't go back down!"

"So *you're* not stuck up," said Amelia Bedelia. "The bridge is."

"What? Right." Flo had a lot on her mind. "No one can get across. Not the tent people. Not the florist. Not the caterer. Not the cake. Not the musicians. No one."

Amelia Bedelia's mother looked at her sister. "I guess this is one of those disasters that will make your wedding special and unique," she said.

"That's the spirit," said Flo. "Are there any ferries?"

Amelia Bedelia was surprised that Flo still believed in fairies. Was she expecting a fairy godmother to help her out somehow?

"Not for a hundred years," said Aunt Mary. "But let me call Bob. He might have an idea."

Bob did have an idea. He told Flo to have everyone meet up at Crusty's Crab Shack on the other side of the bridge. He and Amelia Bedelia's father would arrange a boat to ferry them across the channel and leave them at the pier closest

to Aunt Mary's beach house.

Jason had an idea too. He made some emergency calls to his friends and asked them to contribute food from their restaurants and snack stands in case the caterer didn't make it.

Just as Jason hung up the phone, it rang again. "It's a Mrs. May," said Jason, handing the phone to his mother.

"That's our justice of the peace," said Aunt Mary. "Luckily for us, she lives on *this* side of the bridge."

But when Aunt Mary hung up, she had to sit down.

"What's wrong?" asked Amelia Bedelia's mother.

"She has food poisoning," said Mary.

"She's sick in bed."

"You need someone official to marry you," said Grandma.

"Otherwise you're not really married," said Granddad.

Flo closed her eyes. "Go with the Flo, go with the Flo, go with . . ."

Amelia Bedelia closed her eyes too. "Go with the Flo, go—"

BAAAAAAAAHHHHNNN!!! sounded a boat horn, very near by.

BAAHNN!

Chapter 12

Something Borrowed, Something Blew

They all raced outside to see the *Reel Busy* coming alongside the pier at the marina near Aunt Mary's cottage.

The deck was jammed with musicians and caterers and florists and waiters. There was a large arch made of vines, and a grill and coolers and musical instruments and balloons.

Sailors who normally spent their days baiting hooks and cleaning fish were now unloading fragile floral displays and transporting them to the beach. Deckhands who kept the *Reel Busy* shipshape were now hauling baskets of gourmet food and delicacies onto the pier and on toward the house.

When Bob hopped off the *Reel Busy*, Aunt Mary gave him a huge hug, even though it was bad luck to see him before the wedding. What was a little more bad luck now?

"I figured we'd get Flo's folks over here to set up first," he said. "The guests are starting to arrive too, so I left Crusty and his Crab Shack crew and Amelia Bedelia's father with trays of snacks to hold them over until we can go back for them."

Aunt Mary tried to tell Bob the news. "Mrs. May—"

"That was a lucky break, huh?" said Bob. "Thank goodness Captain Will lives right down the road."

"Mrs. May had to cancel," Aunt Mary said. "She's sick."

Bob took off his baseball cap. Running his fingers through his hair, he said, "So we're out of luck after all? No wedding unless an official performs the ceremony and signs the marriage license, right?"

"Right," said Aunt Mary.

"Right," said Flo.

Amelia Bedelia was watching Captain Will

112

at work. "Go with the Flo, go with the Flo," she whispered to herself. Captain Will was directing one of the ship's cargo booms, lifting something big out of the hold and onto the pier. The object was wrapped in canvas and labeled KEEP FROZEN.

Amelia Bedelia thought that Captain Will was acting pretty official. He certainly *looked* official. Could Captain Will marry people? She wasn't sure if she had dreamed that or if she just wished that it was true. Then she remembered.

"What about your favorite movie, the one we watched at the party? The one with those couples on the cruise ship," said Amelia Bedelia. "The captain married them. Isn't a captain of a ship an official?" They all looked at one another, then over at Captain Will.

Flo bent down and gave Amelia Bedelia a hug that lifted her off her feet. "Sweetheart," she said. "You can go with the Flo anytime."

"You're lucky I have cold storage for fish!" said Captain Will as he approached the group. "Otherwise, this would've melted. What is it?"

"An ice sculpture," said Flo. "For later. Now listen to us."

Bob and Mary explained their situation. They asked Captain Will if he would be so good as to marry them. His face crinkled as he broke out in a belly laugh. "First you borrow my boat, and now you want to borrow me?" he asked. "Unfortunately, captains can't really do that! But I happen to be ordained to perform weddings—I got the papers when my brother was getting married!"

"Sounds like fate," said Flo.

"No . . . it's that old saying!" said Amelia Bedelia. "Aunt Mary already has something old and something new. You and your boat are what she's borrowing."

"Too bad the *Reel Busy* isn't painted blue," said Amelia Bedelia's mother.

BAAHHH! BAAAAAAAHHHNNN!!! sounded the horn, to signal Captain Will that it was time to go pick up the guests. He climbed back aboard the *Reel Busy*. *BAAAAAHHHNNN!!!* Captain Will signaled, blowing the horn and getting under way.

"The trim on his boat is red," said Amelia Bedelia. "But his horn definitely blew."

BAAAAAAAAHHNNN!

116

"Hey, guys," said Amelia Bedelia's father. "Why are you standing around? Don't you have a wedding to put on?"

"How did you get here?" said Amelia Bedelia's mother. "Aren't you feeding snacks to Mary's guests?"

"Charles Lindbergh dropped me off on his way to Paris," Amelia Bedelia's father said airily. Amelia Bedelia had learned in school who Lindbergh was, which was why she did not believe her dad.

Charles Lindbergh

"Is the drawbridge down?" asked Bob.

117

"Nope, the drawbridge is up," said Amelia Bedelia's father.

"So the bridge is up?" said Aunt Mary.

"No, the bridge is down," he said.

"Up, down, sideways," said Flo. "If he's here, the bridge is fixed!"

Chapter 13

Half Hitch + Half Hitch = Totally Hitched

Some things were actually going right. The weather was glorious, the flowers were gorgeous, and the ocean was as smooth as a mirror, reflecting little puffy white clouds that looked like a flock of lambs.

"Maybe that hurricane they were forecasting won't happen, after all," said Amelia Bedelia's father.

"What?" said Aunt Mary.

"Stop joking," said Amelia Bedelia's mother. "I am down to my last nerve."

"What could go wrong now?" asked Amelia Bedelia's father.

As much as Amelia Bedelia loved asking questions, she knew that asking a question like that was like asking for trouble.

Everyone had taken off their shoes

to walk in the sand, except Aunt Mary. "I am wearing these heels—they're my something-new charm," she said. "I can't afford any more bad luck at this point."

That's when Aunt Mary turned around and came face-to-face with the same young woman she'd seen with Bob at the café. Aunt Mary's mouth dropped open and her eyes grew large.

The young woman hugged Mary and said, "Hi, I'm Anita. I haven't had a chance to congratulate you and Uncle Bob. I'm so glad you two found each other."

"Uncle Bob?" said Mary.

"Bob's brother Tom is my father," Anita said. "I love your dress."

"Oh, thank you!" said Aunt Mary. "I'm so happy to meet *you!*"

Everyone was ready. The guests had gathered, and even Amelia Bedelia was amazed at how official Captain Will looked. His dark blue jacket had four gold stripes at the bottom of each sleeve. Those, and his white hat with gold braid, showed he was indeed a captain. He was

carrying the *Nautical Rules of the Road*, making him appear even more serious.

Bob strode down what would have been the aisle, if they weren't at the beach. Following him was the groom's party of Tom—the best man—and Jason and Amelia Bedelia's father.

Then the bridesmaids walked down the aisle—first Aunt Wanda and then Amelia Bedelia's mother, the matron of honor. Amelia Bedelia had never seen

her mother look so beautiful. She kept staring after her and did not move until Flo gave her a prod from behind. "Your turn, kiddo."

Amelia Bedelia wore a dress that Aunt Wanda had found for her at a different vintage shop. It was gauzy and white, with tiny flowers sewn all over it. She wore a little wreath on her head, covered in wildflowers, with four

124

long strands of different-colored ribbons tied to it, trailing down her back.

Amelia Bedelia carried a bucket filled with blossoms, and she began tossing them on the beach, making a path for Aunt Mary. Aunt Mary was supposed to be following her, but when Amelia Bedelia arrived at Captain Will, she turned to see Aunt Mary struggling with her wedding dress.

All the guests turned, looking for the bride. When she saw her, Amelia Bedelia quickly circled around to help her aunt. Flo was pulling on the ends of the big bow that held up the dress. Amelia Bedelia heard a big *RRRRIIIIIPPPPP*!!!

"Oh, great," said Aunt Mary. "This dress was not built for the stresses of modern life," said Flo.

"Neither was I," said Aunt Mary. "My stomach is in knots."

In an instant, Amelia Bedelia knew just what to do. She took the wreath off her head and yanked off the ribbons. She tied them together, end to end. Then, facing Mary, she looped the ribbon over Mary's head, crossed in front and circled both ends behind her. Then Amelia Bedelia tied the only knot she knew, the one she could tie with one hand and her eyes closed. She took a round turn around Mary's waist, securing it with two half hitches.

"You're good to go," said Amelia
Bedelia, sticking her finger into the knot,
testing it with a tug.

When Aunt Mary heard "go," away
she went, with Amelia Bedelia's finger
stuck in the knot.

Quickly, Amelia Bedelia scooped up

her bucket and began tossing blossoms
behind her with her free hand. Most of
the guests assumed it was part of the
ceremony, but Captain Will knew better.
When Aunt Mary and Amelia Bedelia
arrived at the flowered arch, Captain Will
stepped forward to see if he could help.

He spied the knot and understood the situation.

"A round turn with two half hitches," he said, loosening the knot just enough for Amelia Bedelia to slip her finger out. "Nice job, young lady!"

Captain Will cleared his throat. "Mary and Bob, your wedding day has been filled with hitches, everything from a broken bridge to an ill justice of the peace. Hitches such as these might have sunk another couple. But with the support of your families and your sense of humor, you stayed on course. Sometimes a hitch is good. It builds character and commitment. Even a couple of half hitches can come in handy."

He winked at Amelia Bedelia. "After a day like today, it will be my privilege to pronounce you two totally hitched."

Everyone laughed and applauded and cheered. Not one person thought that the best hitch was still to come.

Chapter 14

A Familiar Ring to It

It was time for Aunt Mary and Bob to exchange vows and rings. Tom, the best man, handed Aunt Mary's ring to Bob, and he slid it onto Aunt Mary's finger.

Then Aunt Mary turned to Amelia Bedelia's mother for Bob's ring.

"I was afraid of losing it," said Amelia Bedelia's mother to her sister. "So I stuck it on my thumb. Now it's stuck, really stuck."

Amelia Bedelia wondered why her mother had *stuck* it on her thumb instead of just putting it there. She looked out at the guests, who were whispering and craning their necks to see what was causing the delay. She spotted Pearl and shrugged her shoulders.

Amelia Bedelia's mother and Aunt Mary tried to get the ring off by twisting, pulling, and pushing it back and forth, but it was no use. "My thumb is so swollen that it's never coming off," said Amelia Bedelia's mother.

Suddenly Flo appeared out of nowhere, with a big bottle of bright

blue dishwashing liquid. She squirted it all around the ring.

"Go with the Flo!" she said, pressing her thumbnails under the edge of the ring, urging it to "Give up, already!"

SQUELCH! went the ring, arcing high into the air. Bob nearly caught it but bobbled it. Amelia Bedelia's

father nearly caught it too, but the ring fell into the sand at their feet. Jason scrambled for it but instead covered it up completely.

"Where did it go?" asked Aunt Mary.

Everyone looked and dug and looked, but it was hopeless.

"We'd have a better chance of finding a doubloon," said Jason.

Aunt Mary said, "Bob, you wouldn't happen to have your—"

"In the trunk of my car," said Bob. "Back in a jiffy."

Aunt Mary looked at Amelia Bedelia's

mother. "Did I just get left at the altar?" she asked.

"We all did!" said Amelia Bedelia.

Soon, though, Bob came back down the aisle, scanning the beach with his metal detector. Picking up a signal, he pointed right next to where they had been looking. Jason stuck his hand in the sand, retrieved the ring, and handed it to his mother.

She placed it on Bob's finger without waiting for him to take off his gear.

"I now pronounce you husband and wife!" said Captain Will.

"Let the party begin!" announced Aunt Wanda to the clapping and cheering guests.

The food was incredible. And there was more than enough, since all Jason's friends had shown up with a delicious selection of seaside treats and frosty beverages. Aunt Mary had no trouble convincing them to stay for the party too. But with all the extra guests, they began running out of ice.

"That's plenty of ice right there," said Amelia Bedelia, pointing at the centerpiece. It was a huge

ice sculpture of two interlocking hearts.

"Do you want to break my heart, Amelia Bedelia?" said Flo. "Oh, go ahead. It's going to melt anyway." She handed Amelia Bedelia a small mallet. Clearly she was prepared for almost everything!

"I was stationed on an icebreaker," said Captain Will. "We rescued other ships that had gotten trapped in the ice near the North Pole."

Amelia Bedelia handed the mallet to Captain Will. "You're the expert," she said.

Captain Will whacked the ice sculpture just once, and it shattered

138

into a million ice cubes.

"I may retire," said Flo. "How could I ever top this? Any other wedding would be boring compared to today's."

"You couldn't have planned it better if you'd planned it," said Amelia Bedelia.

Flo laughed and then frowned. She looked at Amelia Bedelia with a puzzled expression.

"Time for a photo!" yelled Amelia Bedelia's father.

"Shake a leg and get yourself over here!" yelled Amelia Bedelia's mother.

Amelia Bedelia and Pearl headed to where Flo was helping a photographer set up a big camera on a tripod. Jason was racing the waves with some beach friends.

Then Amelia Bedelia spotted Anita, Aunt Mary, and Bob looking at a picture together—probably of Blackberry Cottage, because Aunt Mary had a stunned expression on her face. All of a sudden she hugged Bob, and he twirled her around in the air. Aunt Wanda was dancing with Captain Will. It didn't seem as though they were going to stop anytime soon. Grandma and Granddad were eating cake with Bob's family. *Woof! Woof!* And there, racing across the beach at full speed, was Finally. Amelia Bedelia scooped her up.

Flo looked at her Flo chart and shrugged. "Well, the sun is perfect, so let's go with the Flo and just take some photos," she said.

So Amelia Bedelia's mother, Amelia Bedelia's father, Amelia Bedelia, and Finally posed for the photographer. At the very last minute, Amelia Bedelia grabbed Pearl, and her mother grabbed Flo, and Amelia Bedelia's father called out, "Three, two, one! Family hug!"

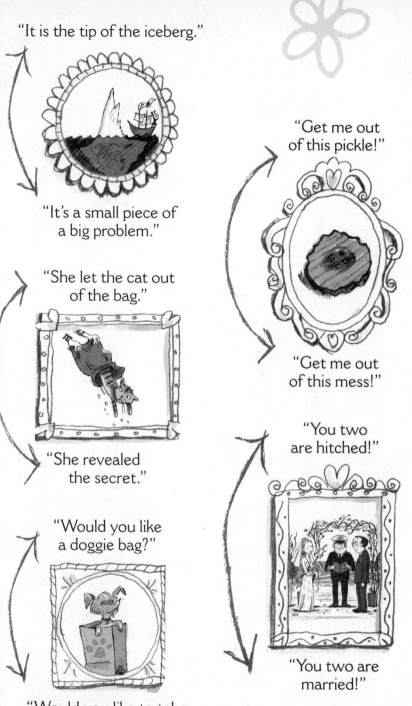

"It is the tip of the iceberg."

"It's a small piece of a big problem."

"Get me out of this pickle!"

"Get me out of this mess!"

"She let the cat out of the bag."

"She revealed the secret."

"You two are hitched!"

"You two are married!"

"Would you like a doggie bag?"

"Would you like to take home the leftover food?"

With
Amelia Bedelia
anything can happen!

Have you read
them all?

#1

Amelia Bedelia wants a new bike—a brand-new shiny, beautiful, fast bike just like Suzanne's new bike. Amelia Bedelia's dad says that a bike like that is really expensive and will cost an arm and a leg. Amelia Bedelia doesn't want to give away one of her arms and one of her legs. She'll need both arms to steer her new bike, and both legs to pedal it.

Amelia Bedelia is going to get a puppy—a sweet, adorable, loyal, friendly puppy! When her parents ask her what kind of dog she'd like, Amelia Bedelia doesn't know what to say. There are hundreds and thousands of dogs in the world, maybe even millions!

#2

#3

Amelia Bedelia is hitting the road. Where is she going? It's a surprise! But one thing is certain. Amelia Bedelia and her mom and dad will try new things (like fishing), they'll eat a lot of pizza (yum), and Amelia Bedelia will meet a new friend—a friend she'll never, *ever* forget.

#4

Amelia Bedelia has an amazing idea! She is going to design and build a zoo in her backyard. Better yet, she is going to invite all her friends to bring their pets and help plan the exhibits and rides.

#5

Amelia Bedelia usually loves recess. One day, though, she doesn't get picked for a team and she begins to have second thoughts about sports. What's so great about racing and jumping and catching, anyway?

Amelia Bedelia and her friends are determined to find a cool clubhouse, maybe even a tree house, for their new club. One day they find the perfect spot—an empty lot with a giant tree. The lot is a mess, so they pitch in and clean it up. And that's when the trouble really begins.

#6

Amelia Bedelia
Cleans Up
by Herman Parish   pictures by Lynne Avril

#7

Amelia
Bedelia
Sets
Sail
by Herman Parish   pictures by Lynne Avril

Amelia Bedelia is so excited to be spending her vacation at the beach! She loves hanging out with her cousin Jason—especially since he's really great at surfing and knows so many kids in town. But one night, Amelia Bedelia sees Jason sneaking out the window. Where is he going? What is he up to?

Amelia Bedelia does not want to take dance classes. She loves to dance for fun, but ballet is not her cup of tea, and she is sure that Dana's School of Dance will be super boring. But guess what? Surprising teachers, new steps, cool kids, and even a pesky ballet bun inspire Amelia Bedelia and her classmates to dance up a storm!

'Amelia
Bedelia
Dances
Off
by Herman Parish   pictures by Lynne Avril

#8

Amelia Bedelia and her classmates are learning about occupations and jobs at school, and that means they go on some really interesting field trips. What does Amelia Bedelia want to be when she grows up? Turns out, the sky's the limit!

Aunt Mary is getting married, and Amelia Bedelia helps with the festivities. She invents a "pop the question" bridal game, helps taste test wedding cakes, and even gets to be the flower girl. But when disaster strikes and threatens to ruin the big day, it's up to Amelia Bedelia to make sure Aunt Mary and Bob tie the knot!

Hooray!

It's a dog's life

It's raining cats and do[g]

The dog ate
my homework